Love In The Time Of Corona

AMY LAURENS

OTHER WORKS

Find other works by the author at www.amylaurens.com

Love In The Time Of Corona

INKLET #96

AMY LAURENS

Inkprint PRESS

www.inkprintpress.com

Print ISBN: 978-1-925825-52-7
eBook ISBN: 9798201835767

www.inkprintpress.com

National Library of Australia Cataloguing-in-Publication Data
Laurens, Amy 1985 –
Love In The Time Of Corona
66 p.
ISBN: 978-1-925825-52-7
Inkprint Press, Canberra, Australia
1. Fiction—Romance—Contemporary 2. Fiction—Romance—Clean & Wholesome

First Print Edition: December 2022
Cover photo © Ed Zbarzhyvetsky via Deposit Photos
Cover design © Inkprint Press
Interior art © Amy Laurens

LOVE IN THE TIME OF CORONA

Thunder rumbled overhead, but one glance and Saria knew there'd be no rain.

There hadn't been for a month, not since the hailstorms, so why would the weather change its mind and start now, vocal complaints aside? She pursed her lips and plunged her hands back into the half-empty basket of wet washing, savouring the coolness against the fierce heat of an evening that smelled dry, full of dust and concrete.

She hung a sock, lilac with two iconic dogs slurping a mutual bowl of spaghetti.

Socks were easy.

Socks were safe.

Saria fastened it to the line with an emerald plastic peg, went back for another sock, hung it with a faded blue peg, breathed deeply.

Thunder rumbled again, a sudden rush of wind racing past, fluttering the spade-shaped leaves on the ornamental pear behind her before disappearing. There was no good reason why it should raise a thrill of fear through her chest, that trailing, sparkling line of adrenalin she'd managed to forget. It did it anyway.

Saria inhaled, reaching for calm, the scent of laundry powder and the faint, lingering traces of vinegar from the wash curling around her.

A shirt next, a soft, white cotton tee. Deftly, Saria grabbed it by the underarm seams and flipped it over the line. A faded red peg on one side.

Her jaw twitched.

The closest peg was another of the green ones. In fact, the next ten or so were green. She'd have to take two steps to the right to reach the closest red peg.

Her jaw twitched again.

Thunder complained softly, dying away into the distance.

Shoulders tense, the taste of her cheek on her tongue as she bit down on it, Saria took the two quick steps, snatched the red peg, and snapped it over the white shirt with a little more force than necessary.

She pressed her eyes closed tightly, left hand curled tight around the rim of the wash basket.

Ten, eleven, twelve... Fourteen. It had been fourteen years since she'd last had this much trouble hanging washing. Heart knocking at her chest,

Saria eyed the remainder of the pegs. There might be enough green ones left to hang everything…

Green pegs. Just focus on the green pens. You can buy another packet tomorrow. It's going to be fine. You'll be fine, they'll be fine… Everyone's going to be fine.

Saria repeated the lie to herself as she hung the rest of the basket, emerald peg after emerald peg after emerald peg.

She ran out of them at the end, but it didn't matter: she'd left the other socks until last, socks and undies and face washers—all the things that could be hung with only a single peg.

She breathed deeply and grabbed up the empty white basket. Fine. Everything was fine.

Dan was out of toilet paper. The realisation came sharply as he reached for the roll in the middle of the night, pulling one, two, three squares free before—tck, tck, rattle—the empty cardboard tube spun fruitlessly on the holder.

He groped around on the floor for the plastic packaging that held his spare rolls—he vaguely understood that some people took them out of the plastic and stacked them neatly in corners and such, and he always aspired to such things, even if they never actually eventuated—but there was naught but crinkling, crackling plastic to meet his fingers.

Despite the heat of the previous afternoon, the early hours of the morning had cooled markedly, and the air drifting in from the bathroom window raised goosebumps over his back.

Well, crap.

Dan snorted at his terrible pun, made the best of what he had, and went back to bed, hands scented with the soft, lingering aroma of the sandal-wood soap. He paused briefly to unlock his phone, squinting at the sudden bright light on his face, and left himself a reminder to hunt down toilet paper in the morning.

Talk about poor timing.

He drifted back to sleep, dreaming of cardboard tubes and empty shelves.

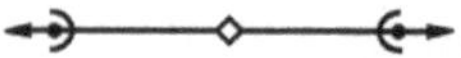

It wouldn't have been so bad, perhaps, Saria mused, if she'd been stuck in a house with other people. But marooned in a two-bedroom town-house alone, she had nothing to distract her from the thoughts rattling around in her head.

And none of her friends or family lived close by; there was no one she could accidentally bump into at the corner store for a bit of much-needed socialisation, no one she could even walk around the block with, exercising while maintaining the strict 'no gatherings of more than two people' rule.

Her sister phoned every second day, her mother twice a week—but it wasn't the same.

It didn't keep the anxiety at bay.

She'd started sleeping with the hallway light on, to be honest. Started jumping at shadows in the dark again, every step toward the bathroom at night a torturous journey of fear clutching at her chest, her breath catching in her throat as the back of her neck prickled with the sense of being stared at.

Morning wasn't much better, these days. Even though it didn't matter in the slightest what she wore—she kept a couple of good blouses by the computer to throw on for zoom meetings and amused herself wondering how many of her colleagues were wearing pyjama pants—the decision of which shirt to put on was turning once more into an agony of indecision. The blue one? The navy? The girl in the golden ballgown reading, or the unicorns with the scarves?

Saria sighed and snagged the unicorn one from the top of the washing pile, wrinkling her nose at the smell of day-old sweat as she pulled it on.

Even that didn't matter these days. No one could get close enough to smell her anyway, and the shirt calmed her down a little.

A liberal spray of rose-scented perfume sweetened the deal, and then she was trotting down the stairs, snagging her wallet off the desk, and slipping into her ballet flats for a quick walk down to the corner store.

The therapist years ago had pointed out that sometimes, the best way to win a battle was to avoid it altogether: if Saria only had green pegs, the anxiety couldn't complain about how she hung her clothes on the line.

(It would probably find another outlet, dealing with it was like playing a protracted game of whack-a-mole, but she'd take the relief where she could find it.)

Outside, she immediately regretted the unicorn shirt decision. Or, not so much that decision specifically as the implicit trust she'd placed in the weather, and the assumption that she wouldn't need her hoodie.

Alack, the weather had betrayed her: the afternoons had been summer-hot the last few weeks, but the nights had been autumn-cold, and this morning it seemed like autumn was finally here to stay.

She inhaled deeply, and the cold air sent long-clawed fingers down to seize her lungs. Urgh. She'd have to go back on her asthma preventer at this rate.

Dan woke to his phone alarm blaring, dragged forcibly to consciousness. He dressed in a daze, vaguely aware somewhere that staying up late every night watching B-grade movies and ordering pizza was going to catch up with him eventually.

With his wallet, if nothing else, because home-delivered pizza wasn't the cheapest meal, and the cafe he'd bought two years ago when he'd moved to Canberra couldn't sustain its business with only take-away orders.

He had enough savings to last him awhile, he was lucky in that regard, but his next paycheque wouldn't be coming in until the end of April when the government welfare payments kicked in.

He paused at the front door of his townhouse, cold morning air drifting over him. That storm front yesterday had done a number on the weather; autumn was apparently here.

Dan snatched up his dark green beanie and crammed it over his loose curls—he'd usually cut them when they got this long, but where was he going to go for the next few months except the grocery store and the government shopfront, and no one at either of those would care about the length of his hair.

These musings took him the first of the three blocks to the tiny shopping complex that served the suburb, and recalculating exactly how long he could make his savings last entertained him the rest of the way.

He had enough money, really. He wasn't in danger of losing his townhouse, wasn't in danger of not being able to eat. He wasn't in the high-risk group for the virus, didn't have any personal contacts who were.

Didn't have many personal contacts at all, really. And that was the point, the thing he kept circling around, working desperately to avoid thinking about.

Because the one thing—the only thing—he was in danger of really was loneliness. Two years, working long hours and weekends to establish the cafe and get it running, playing around writing scripts on the side—because that was what he *really* wanted to do with his life—all of it left him with precious little time to establish any local friendships.

Not that locality mattered any more these days anyway.

Dan entered the small grocery store, the distinctive scent of the air-conditioned air greeting him as he squirted sanitiser on his hands and rubbed it in.

It was tempting to browse, to see if there was anything else he could distract himself with, but he ought to be careful with his money and anyway, toilet paper was a precious commodity and a small distraction might cost him his opportunity.

Sure enough, in the last aisle to the right, opposite the four freezer doors that encased the ice creams and frozen yogurts and sorbets, the toilet paper shelves were empty.

Except…

Dan felt a tiny seed of relief.

One last packet, eight rolls of three-ply, tucked to the side down on the bottom shelf.

Dan took a step closer—

And a woman, shortish, with shiny chocolate-brown hair and a terribly cute grey shirt with four be-scarved unicorns on it crouched down and beat him to it.

His instinct was to lunge at the toilet paper packet. He was out, completely and utterly out and what was he supposed to do? Use a sponge like he was an ancient Roman or something?

The woman glanced up, caught his eye—and something fountained in his chest because holy *crap* she was beautiful—and she was holding the last pack of toilet paper.

Urgh.

"Oh," she said, straightening. "I guess you were after this too?"

He nodded wordlessly.

Something around the corners of her eyes was tight, something in the set of her shoulders—but if she hadn't been holding the last pack of toilet paper, his pack, the packet he really, really needed, he might have stopped breathing there and then.

"I don't even need it, really," she said, eyes over-wide, and he realised the tips of her fingers had blushed white as she gripped the package.

Somehow, it lessened his frustration, and he took half a step back.

"I don't need it," she whispered again, voice thick with misery...

No, something deeper than that. Grief.

Despite himself, Dan's brow wrinkled. "Are you sure?" Because people didn't usually sound like they were grieving at the thought of giving up a few rolls of toilet paper, the absurd situation the world was in right now notwithstanding.

Wordlessly, the woman offered him the package, the plastic crinkling as she held it out to him, gaze averted.

Cautiously, he reached for it. "Normally I wouldn't," he said slowly, to match his gesture. He had the feeling that if he moved too fast right now, she'd spook—and somehow, he didn't want that. "But I really am completely out."

She glanced up at him, a sparkle lurking in her rich brown eyes despite their tightness. "Really?"

Dan nodded. A self-deprecating smile. "Yeah. Ran out right in the middle of the night, too. Super inconvenient." Why was he telling her this? No one, let alone a strange woman in the grocery store, wanted to hear about his toilet paper misadventures. It took everything he had not to wince.

Her lips quirked, an adorable, deep dimple springing to life in her cheek. "You'd better take it then. I have plenty, really."

The relief he felt as she relinquished the package to him was palpable; he breathed easier, his shoulders relaxing as he stood straighter.

She noticed, and a sparkling smile emerged like the sun appearing from behind a cloud.

"So, how many rolls *do* you have?" His mouth had developed a weird kind of sentience of its own, because he would never say something that stupid if he was actually thinking.

But the woman grinned, eyes crinkling adorably. "Twenty-three."

Dan raised his eyebrows. "That's a very precise number."

"I'm a very precise person," she said, still grinning. "Are you really actually out?"

He nodded, a twinge in his stomach.

The woman laughed, and if he'd thought the sun came out before, it was nothing to this. Her laugh was utterly un-self-conscious—utterly infectious. He found himself grinning along, tracing the lines of her mouth with his eyes.

She had great teeth. One of the top ones on the right, first one in from the canine, was a little crooked, but it gave her an adorable air of mischief as she laughed—at him, with him, it didn't matter.

"How on earth did you let yourself run out in a situation like this?" she said, twirling her fingers in the air at the world in general.

A few strands of her long, chocolate-brown hair had fallen over her face, and he found himself longing to reach out and brush it aside.

"I refused to buy in to the panic," Dan said. Brushing his fingers against her face would have been inappropriate even in normal situations, let alone now when it would so flagrantly violate the one-point-five-metre rules.

She nodded along like she knew what he was thinking, shifting her packet of green pegs in the crook of her elbow, the packet crinkling. "You refused to panic buy—which, okay, good on you, I wish I had that kind of self-restraint—only you left it too late and now there's none to be had for love or money, is that it?"

Dan nodded as they effortlessly sidestepped together, making room for a mid-forties man in a suit just on the blue side of navy who came shambling down the aisle, wrapped in a cloud of oblivion and cheap men's cologne, the kind that got into your throat if you breathed too deeply. Dan worked his tongue to clear the taste.

"You know one of the supermarkets in Belconnen has given up entirely?" the woman said, eyes tracking the blue-suited man as he headed back toward the milk. She glanced up and met Dan's gaze briefly, and something warm zipped through him. "Their toilet paper aisle is just full of nappies."

Dan's eyebrows rose. "Well, that's one solution I guess."

A pause, then she snorted in amusement. "Guess so."

A crack of thunder interrupted the conversation.

Dan glanced around, surprised to note that the store did seem to have grown dim, the fluorescent lights taking on the kind of brightness they only got when robbed of daylight.

Dammit. Oh well. At least the toilet paper came in a plastic wrapping. It would get home dry and unharmed, even if he didn't.

The sudden realisation that the lovely woman with the pegs was breathing fast hit him, and he refocused on her. "Hey, are you okay?"

"Yeah, I just walked up is all," she said, and threw him a strained smile. "Hope it doesn't rain." Abruptly, she turned and headed for the cash registers at the front of the store.

He followed, because he needed to pay for his toilet paper—and definitely not because she looked worried, seemed unsettled all of a sudden, and he wanted to make sure she was okay.

Flirting in the toilet paper aisle. Saria shook her head. Had you ever heard of anything more ridiculous?

Still, she couldn't *quite* conceal the little smile that begged to be let out through her pursed lips as the man with the toilet paper—The Man With The Toilet Paper—joined the queue behind her, standing, like her, on his allotted white square, the ones management had taped to the floor, bearing the words "Queue 1.5m Apart".

Usually, Saria would be disappointed at herself for giving in, yet again, to her burgeoning anxiety and visiting the toilet paper aisle at all.

Twenty-three rolls was more than enough to last her, the single occupant of her house, for several weeks, if not more.

(It occurred to her that she didn't actually *know* how long it took her to go through a packet of toilet paper, and the anxiety reared its head: these days, that seemed like a crucial detail to be aware of. She'd have to create a calendar tracker or something.)

Saria shook her head firmly, disguising it to any watching eyes as a way to toss her hair from her shoulders.

Enough.

She had the pegs, that would avoid that outlet. She was a grown woman and there was no one else in the house to complain if she wandered around with lights on a nighttime, even for a brief trip to the bathroom (even if it did feel like losing, most nights).

And everyone in the world was supposed to be washing their hands continuously these days, so even if that *had* been the key factor that had unburied the anxiety she'd worked long years to make peace with, it was, in these days, an utter necessity.

But she wasn't going to beat herself up about the toilet paper.

Struck by the sudden reminder that she hadn't cleaned her hands since she'd used the sanitiser at the entrance of the store, Saria shifted uncomfortably on her square. Her hands felt too dry, too large—too unclean, covered with whatever invisible filth she might have picked up by touching things in the store.

To be fair, she'd only touched the peg packet and the toilet paper, though so had the man… But no, she'd given *him* the package, he was bearing *her* germs and not the other way around.

Saria glanced behind her to where the man who, even at a distance of one-point-five metres, carried the faint scent of soap and something creamy that reminded her of vanilla, but softer, more subtle. It was, she had to admit, an extremely comforting smell.

And something about the way his long, strong fingers danced around the handle of the black shopping basket, the way his brown hair curled out from under the hunter-green beanie—he'd been sensible enough to check the weather before he left, unlike Saria herself—the soft, dark growth of hair over his strong, slightly concave chin and his cheeks that was either three days of refusing to shave or else a carefully manicured short beard, she couldn't quite tell…

Saria's lips twitched. He was watching her.

He'd glanced away as soon as she'd looked at him, fast enough that she couldn't prove it was her he'd been looking at—but the air of studied nonchalance as he thoroughly inspected the little fridge of flavoured milks that stood by one of the registers, radiating cold and humming gently, gave him away.

Saria grinned. "Thirsty?"

He glanced at her, eyebrows shooting up again—it was pretty cute, the way they seemed to do that whenever he was surprised or amused—but expression carefully blank. "Sorry?"

She tilted her head toward the small fridge. "Thirsty?"

He blushed.

Heaven help him, he actually blushed. Saria couldn't help it; her grin widened.

Thunder rolled, interrupting, and her happy moment was quenched as suddenly as the downpour that started outside. She frowned at the view beyond the automatic glass doors of the shop's entrance as heavy, fat raindrops splattered onto the concrete. The ground was drenched in seconds, not a dry corner left beyond the eaves of the building.

Anxiety palpated at her heart.

It's okay, she told herself through clenched jaw. *There's plenty of air circulating in here, you can wait it out for a bit without getting sick. It's going to be fine.* She fumbled for her phone in her pocket, pulling up the BOM site to check the rain radar.

"How's it looking?" the cute man said, somehow managing to peer over her shoulder without actually getting any closer.

Saria flashed the screen at him: a broad band of red and yellow moving east, large patches of blue and white following in its wake.

"Urgh. Good for the farmers," he said, "but I guess we'll be stuck here while it passes."

Saria's jaw twitched again.

The person in front of her moved up to the next square in line.

Saria followed suit, and the man moved up behind her too.

The rain gushed down, pounding the roof, white noise turned up to fifty. Her stomach was knotting, her grip on the pegs too tight. Stupid, to have risked coming out to get them. Should have stayed home.

Pegs weren't really urgent or essential, anyway. Maybe this was just punishment for bending the rules.

If she'd stayed home this morning, she would have gone nuts.

More nuts, she amended.

But being stuck in the smallish grocery store for an hour while the rain passed wasn't exactly going to be good for her mental health either. There was only one door. Not everyone was using the hand sanitiser provided as they walked in. There was nowhere clean to sit, nowhere that wasn't risking exposure, risking her mother's health…

Saria pressed her eyes closed. *It's fine. I'll get Hannah to check in on Mum for the next fourteen days, just to be safe. They have air-conditioning in here, the air's being cycled through.*

They probably don't have medical-grade filters.

There aren't that many people here anyway, maybe twenty, thirty of us in the whole store including employees. Just keep your distance, have a shower and change your clothes when you get home. You'll be fine. Mum'll be fine.

Cute Hat Guy—Shoot, when had she given him a moniker? Did she really feel that much of a spark between them, or was she just starved for human company?—cleared his throat gently behind her.

Saria glanced around, realised the person in front of her had finished paying for their goods, stepped forward and laid her pack of pegs on the counter with a crinkle diminished by the roaring of the downpour on the roof.

Her chest was tight, and it was impossible to tell if it was asthma or anxiety—or covid, obviously, but that was a long shot option.

Her anxiety reminded her it *was* still an option, though, as she tapped her bank card on the pay terminal, declined a receipt, and re-collected her pegs sans shopping bag.

She went to the glass doors mostly out of habit, and stood for a long moment watching the rain fall.

There were already some small puddles, there in the corner of the square of fake grass, over there by the bike rack out front of the take-away store, and along the edge of the path by the restaurant in the corner, its clear plastic awning drawn tightly closed, the up-turned chairs inside made ghostly by the combination of rain and awning.

Garlic bread. Abruptly, she was craving garlic bread.

"What are you going to do?" Cute Hat Man had joined her at the doors— 'joined her' in the loose, one-point-five-metre sense of the world these days.

Saria shrugged. "I'm not really dressed for it." She could stick under the awning around the side of the little shopping complex—to the left, it joined up with the take-away store, and if she turned left again it ran down past the hairdresser and the beauty parlour, all the way to the cafe—but after that? Her shirt would be soaked through before she crossed the first road. And it was four blocks to home.

And, she added with a shiver as one of them stepped a little too close to the automatic doors and they shushed open, letting in a blast of frigid air, it was freezing.

Goosebumps rose immediately on her bare arms. She cuddled the packet of pegs to her so that she could rub at her biceps.

If she ran home in the rain, she'd be soaked and frozen and would probably at the very least end up with an asthma attack from the cold, damp air. If she stayed here, her anxiety would spiral. But her chances of catching anything—*logically*—were very small.

Cute Hat Man was eyeing her up, a considering sort of weight in his gaze.

He leaned forward to peer through the glass doors—they opened again, admitting another blast of chilled air that made the air-conditioning inside the grocery store seem positively cozy—and glanced back at her. "We're not supposed to linger anywhere else," he said, somewhat inexplicably.

What did he expect her to do? Was he judging her for choosing to stay here and weather out the storm rather than running home in the rain? His tone didn't seem quite right for that, but...

"I'll be back," he said, and he ducked outside.

Saria blinked.

The large bottle of clear hand sanitiser on its stand by the doors caught her eye. Sighing, she took the single step toward it, used the edge of her hand to squirt some into one palm, and rubbed it liberally over her hands.

A couple of other customers finished paying for their goods and hovered uncertainly around the entrance nearby.

Too nearby. There were three others, four, five…

And then the oblivious man in his almost-navy suit and 1950s slicked-back hairdo rambled through the middle of all of them, unconscious or uncaring about everyone shifting to make room for him, and stopped right in front of the glass doors so they opened and stayed that way while he surveyed the outdoors.

Saria's chest was getting tighter. She gulped at the air, but couldn't get it all the way down to the bottom of her lungs, couldn't quite catch her breath, like she was breathing through a heavy woollen blanket. The cold scent of wet concrete and moist air funnelled down her throat, stinging, biting, and that hand full of long claws seized in her lungs again.

She coughed, took a few steps away from the doors, clutched at the un-sealed wooden edge of the stand that held the on-sale fruit and veggies. She closed her eyes, inhaling slowly, even-ly. The tomato-scented air still didn't reach the bottom of her lungs, but that didn't matter, she wouldn't suffocate, this had happened thousands of times before and she'd never died from it yet, never passed out from lack of oxygen, everything was fine, it was all fine, she was going to be okay.

"Hey," a soft, male voice said. "Are you okay?"

Cute Hat Man, eyes full of concern, body angled toward her while keeping his distance. In his hands, two silver loaves, long and thin. Garlic bread, from the take-away.

"Yeah," Saria said tightly. "Just…" Which was it? Too many people? Be-ing stuck here because of the rain? The suited man—gone, now, she realised, of course he hadn't walked to the store in his suit like that, he must have decided a brief foray into the rain was worth it to get back to his Lexus or Audi or something so he could go straight home rather than being stuck here with the riffraff—the suited man had been a trigger, but these days, that wasn't saying much.

These days, hanging laundry with mismatching pegs could set her off.

Saria sighed, tried to offer this kind, concerned stranger a smile. "I'm OK," she said. "Just a panic attack."

Crap. She hadn't meant to admit to that. She watched for the light in his eyes to dim like it often did when she confessed her dirty secret to people—but his expression just softened.

"Here," he said, offering one of his silver loaves to her. "You seemed cold."

Unbelievable. She hadn't voiced her desire for garlic bread, had she, when she'd stood by the door a few minutes ago? She was sure she hadn't. "You really didn't have to do that," she said as the sharp, savoury scent twined around her.

He smiled, and it was just a little shy. "You seemed cold," he said again, jiggling the foil-wrapped gift at her.

Her breath was stuck—and not, for once, because of asthma or anxiety.

Heart pitter-pattering, Saria reached for the little loaf, so warm in her fingers, nestled in its armour of wrinkled foil. "Thank you," she breathed.

Another couple of shoppers finished paying for their groceries and joined the burgeoning crowd at the door.

Saria side eyed them, took half a step away.

"Come on," said Cute Hat Man. "Let's head down the back, I think there was a pallet of canned corn they might not mind us perching on."

Saria followed after him, if only to

get away from the people by the front door. "What's your name?" she asked as she debated the merits of breaking open the garlic bread loaf. (Pro: Garlic bread. Delicious. Con: She hadn't washed her hands.)

"Dan. You?"

She'd sanitised. Her anxiety would just have to live with that. "Saria."

He glanced back at her. "Beautiful."

Her breath caught. She wasn't quite sure if he meant her name—or her. Either way, a little frisson ran through her stomach, trailing and sparking in the same way anxiety did—but this time, entirely pleasant.

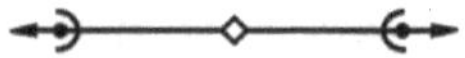

"So why pegs?" Dan asked as he led Saria to the back corner of the store, away from the rain, away from the people that had seemed to trigger her panic. Oh, bugger. "Wait, don't answer that. You don't need to answer that," he said hurriedly as they reached the pallet of corn.

"It's okay," she said quietly as she inspected the pallet. "It's the anxiety." She flicked him a quick sideways glance. "It's been okay for years, manageable at least, but all this…" She did that hand twirl again that she'd done earlier. "It's flaring up. Washing my hands all the time started it, I think. It's too close to the kinds of symptoms I used to have when I was younger anyway." Saria sat on the pallet with a heavy sigh. "It's stupid. Really stupid," she added with an apologetic look.

He sat as beside her as he could. "I'm not judging," he said, and unwrapped the end of his garlic bread, both because it was the obvious thing to do and so it didn't seem like he was focusing on her too much.

"I can't hang clothes out with different coloured pegs," she said, tossing her head like she either expected him to criticise her for it, or because she was already criticising herself. Following his lead, she unwrapped her loaf of garlic bread, pulled off the crust, and stuffed it into her mouth.

"That sucks," Dan said, his own crust poised halfway to his mouth, the thick, melty butter dripping down his index finger. One of his best mates in high school had had anxiety, badly. A couple of times it had been touch and go, and Dan still occasionally had nightmares about the time Matt had had a panic attack right before an exam in their senior year.

They'd been seventeen, and Dan had never witnessed anything so scary in his life up till that point.

He frowned, remembering how shy Matt had been around strangers. "You don't seem like the kind of person who'd have anxiety." He shoved the crust in his mouth, then turned to

Saria, wide-eyed. "Sorry, I didn't mean like I don't believe you or anything, that wasn't what I—"

"It's fine," she cut in, cradling her garlic bread in her lap. "I know what you mean. A lot of people assume anxiety means social anxiety, and yet I talk to strangers just fine." She raised her loaf at him, a kind of salute. "People don't make me anxious. I like people. It's my own thoughts that send me spiralling." She tapped a finger to the side of her forehead.

Dan felt his eyebrows tighten. "But just now, at the front..." He tilted his head toward the front of the shop.

Saria smiled wryly. "It's not the people. It's corona."

"Ah." He gave a slow nod. Rustled in his foil for another piece of garlic bread, tore it in half, popped the soft, pillowy top part of the slice into his mouth.

Mmm. Best decision of the week.

Second best, maybe. Talking to Saria had surely been the first, though if he hadn't gotten the garlic bread he wouldn't have got to talk to her as much, so. A tie, maybe.

"How did you know I was craving garlic bread?" Saria asked, and he realised she was nearly halfway done with her loaf.

Dan's eyebrows lifted. "I didn't. But you really did look freezing, and you seemed... tense. I, uh." The sentence stuttered to a halt. *I what? I wanted to make you smile again? I wanted to make you feel better?* None of those were normal, acceptable things to say to a woman you'd literally just met in the toilet paper aisle of the local grocery store.

She smiled though. Not a tight, self-deprecating one, or that sparkling, teasing grin like she'd given him before. This was a gentle, warm expression. Made him feel like she approved of him, like he was the best human alive, just for a second, just for now.

"You know," he said. "Under normal circumstances, I might ask you out on a date after this."

Saria grinned, that infectious, sparkling one she'd given him earlier. "Under normal circumstances, I might have agreed."

Dan shifted on the pallet, angling himself a little more toward her. "So what? We appreciate this for what it is and let it go?" *I could ask for her phone number. Would that be too much?* He couldn't bear the thought of scaring her off, even loneliness was better than that.

Saria shook her head. "Don't be ridiculous. I'm lonely as heck these days and the anxiety spirals just make it worse. Here, I'll give you my number."

Just like that.

He was floating.

"Also," she said, "I usually come here on Thursday mornings." Eyes alight with mischief, she popped a slice of garlic bread into her mouth, licking the tip of her finger.

Dan's heart double-timed. "I've never dated from two meters away before."

She shrugged. "Has anyone?"

True.

And Saria was getting out her phone, her deliciously pink tongue tip licking garlic butter away from the corner of her mouth, and she gave him her number, and he gave her his, and despite the prohibition on social gatherings, they were in the grocery store so it was all okay, and they finished their garlic bread and laughed and swapped isolation stories, and the rain gifted them the very best half hour he could have dared to imagine.

THE MAKING OF
LOVE IN THE TIME OF CORONA

I wrote this story 'live', as it were, while living the context of the story. It was for a course I was doing (online; weren't they all at that time?) and it was the first time I'd been categorically told that I wasn't allowed to use magic or tech to fix things.

Write contemporary?! No magic?! No technology?! Nothing???!!

Naturally, I decided to write a romance instead, because at least that's genre fiction (and I'm terrible at mysteries or crime when I don't have speculative elements to lean on) and I'd had experience writing romance plots and subplots in my other work.

As it turned out, the key to writing contemporary was to steal large parts of my own life, twist it into a romance, and call it done.

Although neither of these characters are me, we did indeed nearly run out of toilet paper because we refused to panic buy during the early stages of the disease's invasion of our country; one supermarket did replace its toilet paper aisle with nappies; and Saria's anxiety is intimately familiar.

Like Saria, compulsions that I hadn't experienced in years began to resurface around the time of Covid-19, triggered in large part by the constant need for handwashing—even though handwashing has never been part of my compulsions.

The pegs, though? And the inordinate fear of the dark? Yep. Those are very, very familiar when my anxiety is at its peak. Which thankfully, these days, is not too terribly often.

And Saria gets her happy ending, at least for now, which just goes to show: anxiety doesn't get to dictate your life. Because you are still a person, and no matter what anxiety says, you are not a failure, and you are always worthy of love.

Read more by Amy Laurens!

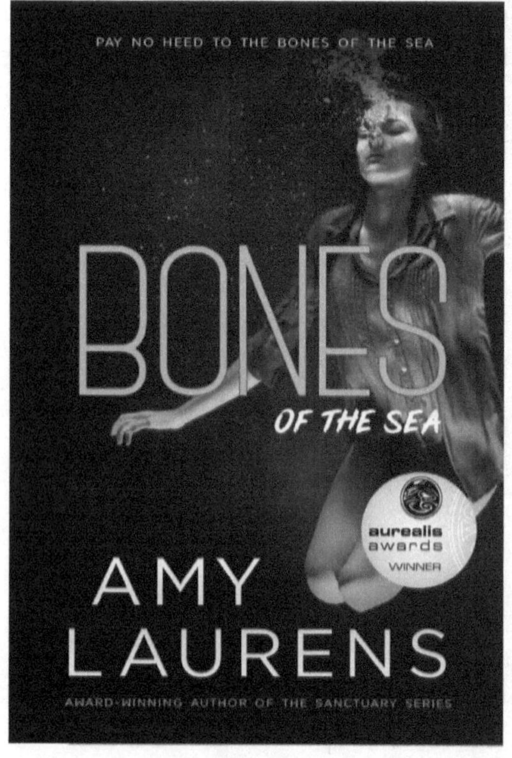

BONES OF THE SEA

THE MAN—WHOSE NAME IS IRRELEVANT, FOR HE shall soon be dead—wandered down the beach where sand whiter than any he'd seen before swashed between a short, head-high cliff to his left, and the frothing waves of the ocean to his right. Salt filled the air, but below that, something else lingered, and he couldn't quite place his… nose… on what it was.

Of course, the locals were horrified that he was here at all. But he was a Man Of Learning, and was not accustomed to heeding the warnings of people obviously less learned than himself, especially when they spoke tales of a beach that left no trespasser alive.

He'd scoffed. Ridiculous, their legends of a beach where to set one toe on the sand was to seal your own death sentence before the rising of the next full moon.

He was far more interested in analysing the sand, quite literally whiter than any he'd seen before, and thus far resistant to his attempts to decode it. He'd thought a pure variety of quartz before he'd arrived, but upon reaching the beach, pulling into the little deserted cul-de-sac dead end festooned with warning signs ('Cursed Beach, Do Not Enter'; 'Beware The Bones Of The Sea'), he'd switched his engine off, opened the car door to the sound of waves and wind through the saltbush, and he'd seen the sharp drop-off down to the sand and had changed his mind to chalk, or maybe gypsum.

But there'd been no tiny fossils his portable microscope could detect, and the sand, whatever it was made from, had failed to fizz under the application of a drop of acid from his little glass vial, so that struck gypsum and chalk from the list of options.

Now, after several hours on the beach to no avail as the hot evening sun seared his hands and the light glinting off both ocean and white sand blinded him, he'd had enough. He'd run out of fresh water, ideas, and patience all, and was presently hiking back around the cove to his car that glinted silver and tantalising at the far end of the beach, a haven of cool air and fresh water.

Stay. Stay a little while longer.

The salt clung to his skin, filming his lips, the inside of his nose, the back of his throat. Somehow, the ocean smelled sharper here, more concentrated. Briefly, he wondered if that was the source of the townsfolk's rumours; but a higher salt concentration ought to have meant people floated better, drowned less. No. There must simply be a convergence of factors that meant the currents here were particularly treacherous, and indeed, casting his gaze out to the distant horizon, examining the interplay of wave and off-white foam, the cove did seem to be quite swirly, with a few smooth tracts he thought were probably rips.

As ever, folklore had a logical series of explanations behind it.

Just a little longer.

His leather sandal caught on something in the sand.

He stumbled.

Ow. That hurt.

Whatever it was, it had poked through the holes in his footwear to stab at his toes.

Glaring, impatient, our nameless victim kicked away some of the strange, defiant white sand—and inhaled sharply.

Once the initial burst of adrenalin subsided—something a surprise human skull will inevitably inspire,

regardless of one's general compo-
sure—it seemed obvious.

Of course. The one thing he hadn't
tested for was bone.

So focused on unlocking the mys-
tery of the sand's composition was he
that his initial reaction was deep, glee-
ful satisfaction.

Dawning understanding, however,
made him lift his feet, hesitantly at
first, shaking the white sand—bone—
sand, think of it as sand, it's safer that
way—but it's bone, really it's bone, it's
all bone, every single grain of it, pure
white, sun-bleached bone, spat up
from the guts of the ocean the way a
predatory owl spits out the bones of its
prey—and then his feet were dancing,
just like his stomach, as he leapt for
the cliff and tried to haul himself up
and off the beach because God, oh
God, he was standing on bones and
only bones, and the skull he'd uncov-
ered had been human, and there, just

down the beach, that rock wasn't a rock, it was another skull, and oh God, how many people had died here?

He realised the sobbing was his, rasps of panic as he scrabbled at the embankment that should have been easier to climb than it was, his fingers digging at the rock, skin tearing, sandals scraping for purchase…

Stay.

His back was to the ocean when the freak wave rose, a local tsunami of salt and hunger.

It smashed into him.

As it dragged him out to sea, all he felt was cold, so bitter it froze his bones right in his body.

An hour later, as the sun spilled red-orange lifeblood out over the ocean, the ocean spat a skull, bleached-white and grinning, back up onto the beach. A moment later, as the full moon crested over the craggy headland behind, a sternum—*most* of its ribs still attached—joined the skull, followed a moment later by a single scapula.

And as the moon rose and the ocean swallowed the sun, a whisper began that sounded like the wind… until you realised there was nothing but saltbush for the wind to disturb, and the whispers sounded strangely like a voice, hungry, crooning, and singing.

Feed me.

Feeed mee.

Feeeed meeeeee….

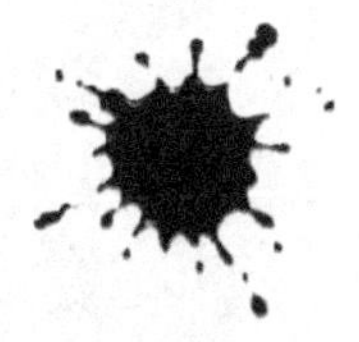

INKLETS

Collect them all! Released on the 1st and 15th of each month.

Dancer, Dreamer
Seer
LIANA BROOKS

As Time
Whirls Slowly
Past
AMY LAURENS

Far More
Satisfying
Than Hell
AMY LAURENS

Just
Another Day
In Hell
LIANA BROOKS

Moon AND
Morning
AMY LAURENS

Some
Impropriety
Expected
AMY LAURENS

NEON SNOW
LIANA BROOKS

Reincarnation
LIANA BROOKS

More Than
Mushrooms
AMY LAURENS

DOUBLE ISSUE
INKLET #092
How To Make A Star
& The World Ended
LIANA BROOKS

INKLET #093
CAUGHT
IN THE ACT
AMY LAURENS

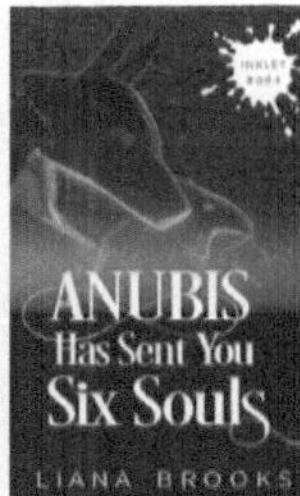
INKLET #094
ANUBIS
Has Sent You
Six Souls
LIANA BROOKS

INKLET #095
PRAYER TO A
GODDESS
LIANA BROOKS

INKLET #096
Love In The
Time Of Corona
AMY LAURENS

INKLET #097
RECRUITMENT
AMY LAURENS

INKLET #098
IDENTITY
Theft 101
LIANA BROOKS

INKLET #099
Curses
With Benefits
AMY LAURENS

INKLET #100
NECROMANCER
TROUBLES
LIANA BROOKS